Temperate Forest Experiments

8 Science Experiments in One Hour or Less

ROBERT GARDNER
ILLUSTRATED BY TOM LABAFF

 **Enslow Publishers, Inc.**
40 Industrial Road
Box 398
Berkeley Heights, NJ 07922
USA
http://www.enslow.com

Copyright © 2015 by Robert Gardner

All rights reserved.

No part of this book may be reproduced by any means without the written permission of the publisher.

Library of Congress Cataloging-in-Publication Data

Gardner, Robert, 1929-
　Temperate forest experiments : 8 science experiments in one hour or less / Robert Gardner.
　　p. cm. — (Last minute science projects with biomes)
　Summary: "A variety of science projects related to the temperate forest that can be done in under an hour, plus a few that take longer for interested students"— Provided by publisher.
　Includes index.
　ISBN 978-0-7660-5922-1
　1. Forest ecology—Experiments—Juvenile literature. 2. Trees—Experiments—Juvenile literature. 3. Science projects—Juvenile literature. I. Title.
　QH541.5.F6G37 2015
　577.3'078—dc23
　　　　　　　　　2013008783

Future editions:
Paperback ISBN: 978-0-7660-5923-8
ePUB ISBN: 978-0-7660-5924-5
Single-User PDF ISBN: 978-0-7660-5925-2
Multi-User PDF ISBN: 978-0-7660-5926-9

Printed in the United States of America
052014 Lake Book Manufacturing, Inc., Melrose Park, IL
10 9 8 7 6 5 4 3 2 1

To Our Readers: We have done our best to make sure all Internet Addresses in this book were active and appropriate when we went to press. However, the author and the publisher have no control over and assume no liability for the material available on those Internet sites or on other Web sites they may link to. Any comments or suggestions can be sent by e-mail to comments@enslow.com or to the address on the back cover.

♻ Enslow Publishers, Inc., is committed to printing our books on recycled paper. The paper in every book contains 10% to 30% post-consumer waste (PCW). The cover board on the outside of each book contains 100% PCW. Our goal is to do our part to help young people and the environment too!

Illustration Credits: Tom LaBaff (www.tomlabaff.com)

Photo Credits: .©1999Artville, LLC, p. 13; David Stephens, Bugwood.org, p. 27 (top left); Paul Wray, Iowa State University, Bugwood.org, p. 42; Shutterstock.com:© cristovao, p. 5; ©Cebas, p. 24; © jaroslava V, p. 25(top); © Ragne Kabanova(birch lumber), p. 27, © Hayati Kayhan(pine lumber), p. 27, © Vladimir Melnik(birch trees), p. 27; © Todd Taulman, p. 31; © Shironin, p. 43(top); © xrender, p. 43(bottom); ©Martin Fowler, p. 44; © 3523studio, p. 45(top); © Alexander Kazantsev, p. 45(middle); © Fotofermer, p. 45(bottom); ©Thinkstock: Lightwriter1949/ iStock, p. 7, roman023/iStock, p. 23; Steven Katovich, USDA Forest Service, Bugwood.org, p. 29

Cover Credits: Shutterstock.com: © Masson (woman); © Labrador Photo Video(Red geranium); ©filmfoto(Green oak leaf); Valentyna7(outdoor thermometer); ©Onur YILDIRIM (clock with yellow arrows); ©Thinkstock: zokru(robin); Maria Wachala/Hemera(green tree)

Contents

Are You Running Late? 4
Temperate Forest Biomes 4
The Scientific Method 8
Science Fairs 9
Safety First 10
A Note About Your Notebook 11

30 Minutes or Less 12
1   Using Maps (20 minutes) 12
🎗 2   A Climatogram of a City (20 minutes) 14
🎗 3   Using a Tree's Shadow to Measure Its Height (30 minutes) 16
🎗 4   Another Way to Measure a Tree's Height (30 minutes) 18
   5   Seasons in a Temperate Forest (30 minutes) 20

One Hour or Less 22
🎗 6   How Old Was That Tree? (1 hour) 22
🎗 7   Leaf Anatomy (1 hour) 24
🎗 8   Testing Wood for Hardness (1 hour) 26

Two Hours or More 28
🎗 9   The Density of Hardwood and Softwood (1 to 2 hours) 28
🎗 10 Chromatography and Leaf Pigments (2 hours) 32
   11 Leaves: A Tree's Food Factory (2 days) 36
🎗 12 Transpiration: How Trees Lose Water in Warm Weather (2 days) 38
🎗 13 Transpiration: Do Trees Lose Water in Cold Weather? (2 days) 40
   14 Trees, Flowers, and Cones (1 to 2 months) 42
🎗 15 Trees, Flowers, Fruits, and Seeds (1 to 2 months) 44

Words to Know 46
Further Reading 47
Index 48

🎗 Contains ideas for more science fair projects.

Are You Running Late?

If you have a science project that is due soon, maybe tomorrow, this book will help you. It has experiments about temperate forest biomes. Many of the experiments can be done in less than one hour. An estimate of the time needed is given for each experiment. Even if you have plenty of time to prepare for your next science project or science fair, you can use and enjoy this book.

Most experiments are followed by a "Keep Exploring" section. There you will find ideas for more science projects. The details are left to you, the young scientist. You can design and carry out your own experiments, under adult supervision, when you have more time.

For some experiments, you may need a partner to help you. Work with someone who likes to do experiments as much as you do. Then you will both enjoy what you are doing. In this book, if any safety issues or danger is involved in doing an experiment, you will be warned. In some cases you will be asked to work with an adult. Please do so. Don't take any chances that could lead to an injury.

Temperate Forest Biomes

A biome is a region of the earth with a particular climate. The plants and animals that live in a biome are quite similar all around the world. This book is about temperate forest biomes. But there are other biomes. Earth's biomes include deserts, tundra, taiga, grasslands, rain forests, and temperate forests.

A temperate forest contains both evergreen and deciduous trees. (Deciduous trees lose their leaves in the winter.) Broad-leafed deciduous trees, such as maples, oaks, hickory, ash, and beech, are common in a temperate forest. The winters are cold and the summers are warm. In winter, the leafless trees do not grow. Without their leaves, trees lose very little water. Growth occurs during the warmer months when leaves are present. It is in the chlorophyll-rich leaves that photosynthesis takes place. Photosynthesis is the process by which plants make food. Leaf cells, using chlorophyll as a catalyst, combine carbon dioxide and water to make food for the plant.

Forests are filled with deciduous trees. The leaves turn colors in the fall and then drop from the trees.

In the fall, as the air cools, the green chlorophyll slowly diminishes. The other pigments—reds, yellows, and oranges—appear. The woodlands glow with color in the autumn sun.

Typically, precipitation falls throughout the year in a temperate forest. With plenty of moisture, shrubs and plants grow beneath the trees. Deeper still, the trees' roots penetrate a moist soil rich in minerals and organic matter supplied by decaying leaves. On the forest floor, and in the trees above, a variety of animals make their homes. There are birds, deer, squirrels, raccoons, opossums, foxes, black bears, rodents, and other animals. Many amphibians, reptiles, and insects also make their home in this biome.

During the winter, some of the forest animals—bats, woodchucks, mice, turtles, and bears—hibernate. They spend the cold months sleeping in caves, dens, or burrows. Their metabolism, heart, and breathing rates all decrease. This reduces their need for food as they snooze the winter away. Their only source of nourishment comes from the fat they develop during an autumn of feasting. Other animals endure the winter by eating berries, nuts, tree bark, twigs, buds, and an assortment of small life forms.

To survive, forest plants and animals require lots of water. A temperate forest receives 30 to 80 inches (75 to 200 cm) of rain per year. The moisture keeps forest humidity at 60 to 80 percent. Unlike a desert biome, the high concentration of moist air is an insulator. It deters heat from entering and leaving the biome. A desert's dry air leads to blistering hot days and chilly nights. But temperatures in a temperate forest insulated by humidity do not fluctuate greatly from day to night.

As the word *temperate* indicates, temperate forests are found in the earth's temperate zone. The northern temperate zone extends from the Tropic of

Cancer (latitude 23.5° north) to the Arctic Circle (66.5° north). A similar zone exists south of the Tropic of Capricorn. But very little deciduous forest is found in the Southern Hemisphere. A look at a world map shows why. Not much land lies south of the Tropic of Capricorn (23.5° south).

There is a large temperate forest in the United States. It extends from a bit west of the Great Lakes eastward to the Atlantic Ocean and southward to the Gulf of Mexico. When the Pilgrims landed in 1620, there were more than a billion acres of forest in what is now the United States. Three hundred years later, one fourth of the trees had been cleared for farming and lumber. Since then, efforts to conserve our temperate forests have added 7.5 million acres of forest.

A temperate forest is layered. Tall trees, such as oaks, maples, hickories, and poplars, form the forest's canopy (roof). Shorter trees form a second shorter layer, the understory. Near the forest floor, we find shrubs such as witch hazel and spice bush. Finally, there is an herb layer containing mushrooms, wild flowers, and other small plants. The floor is covered with dead leaves. The leaves decompose into the minerals and organic matter of the forest soil.

Deer are one of the animals found in the temperate forest.

The Scientific Method

To do experiments the way scientists do, you need to know about the scientific method. It is true that scientists in different areas of science use different ways of experimenting. Depending on the problem, one method is likely to be better than another. Designing a new medicine for heart disease and finding evidence of water on Mars require different kinds of experiments.

Despite these differences, all scientists use a similar approach as they experiment. It is called the scientific method. In most experimenting, some or all of the following steps are used: making an observation, coming up with a question, creating a hypothesis (a possible answer to the question) and a prediction (an if-then statement), designing and conducting an experiment, analyzing results, drawing conclusions about the prediction, and deciding if the hypothesis is true or false.

Scientists share the results of their experiments by writing articles that are published in science journals.

You might wonder how you can use the scientific method. You begin when you see, read, or hear about something in the world that makes you curious. So you ask a question. To find an answer, you do a well-designed investigation; you use the scientific method.

Once you have a question, you can make a hypothesis. Your hypothesis is a possible answer to the question (what you think might be true). For example, you might hypothesize that in a temperate forest autumn colors will appear only after the first frost. Once you have a hypothesis, it is time to design an experiment to test your hypothesis.

In most cases, you should do a controlled experiment. This means having two subjects that are treated the same except for the one thing being tested. That thing is called a variable. For example, to test the hypothesis above, you might compare the appearance of autumn colors in two similar regions. One region would be where there has been a frost. A second region would be one where no frost has occurred. If there were colored trees in the frosted area and none in the region without a frost, you might conclude your hypothesis was true. However, you would probably observe that fall colors appear in most regions well before a frost. So you would have to conclude your hypothesis was not true.

The results of one experiment often lead to another question. In the case above, that experiment might lead you to ask, what then does cause fall colors to appear? Whatever the results, something can be learned from every experiment!

Science Fairs

Some of the investigations in this book contain ideas that might be used as a science fair project. Those ideas are indicated with a symbol (*). However, judges at science fairs do not reward projects or experiments that are simply copied from a book. For example, a diagram of a tree would not impress most judges. However, an experiment to estimate the volume of water that evaporates from a tree in one day would probably attract their attention.

Science fair judges tend to reward creative thought and imagination. It is difficult to be creative or imaginative unless you are really interested in your project. Therefore, try to choose something that excites you. And before you jump into a project, consider, too, your own talents and the cost of the materials you will need.

If you decide to use an experiment or idea found in this book as a science fair project, find ways to modify or extend it. This should not be difficult. As you do investigations, new ideas will come to mind. You will think of questions that experiments can answer. The experiments will make excellent science fair projects, especially because the ideas are yours and are interesting to you.

Safety First

Safety is very important in science. Certain rules should be followed when doing experiments. Some of the rules below may seem obvious to you, others may not, but it is important that you follow all of them.

1. Do any experiments or projects **under the adult supervision** of a science teacher or knowledgeable adult.

2. Read all instructions carefully before proceeding with a project. If you have questions, check with your supervisor before going further.

3. **Always wear safety goggles** when doing experiments that could cause particles to enter your eyes. Tie back long hair and do not wear open-toed shoes.

4. Do not eat or drink while experimenting. Never taste substances being used (unless instructed to do so).

5. Do not touch chemicals.

6. Do not let water drops fall on a hot lightbulb.

7. The liquid in some older thermometers is mercury (a dense liquid metal). It is dangerous to touch mercury or breathe its vapor. That is why mercury thermometers have been banned in many states. When doing experiments, use only non-mercury thermometers, such as digital thermometers or those filled with alcohol. If you have a mercury thermometer in the house, **ask an adult** to take it to a place where it can be exchanged or safely discarded.

8. Do only those experiments that are described in the book or those that have been approved by **an adult**.

9. Maintain a serious attitude while conducting experiments. Never engage in horseplay or play practical jokes.

10. Remove all items not needed for the experiment from your work space.

11. At the end of every activity, clean all materials used and put them away. Then wash your hands thoroughly with soap and water.

A Note About Your Notebook

Your notebook, as any scientist will tell you, is a valuable possession. It should contain ideas you may have as you experiment, sketches you draw, calculations you make, and hypotheses you may suggest. It should include a description of every experiment you do. It should include data you record, such as volumes, temperatures, masses, and so on. It should also contain the results of your experiments, graphs you draw, and any conclusions you make based on your results.

30 Minutes or Less

Here are experiments about temperate forest biomes that you can do in 30 minutes or less. If you need to complete a science project by tomorrow, there's not much time left. So let's get started!

1. Using Maps
(20 minutes)

WHAT YOU NEED:
- map of biomes in Figure 1
- map of the world or large world globe

What's the Plan?
Let's find out where temperate forest biomes are located around the world. And let's find out in which type of biome you live.

What You Do

1. Examine the map in Figure 1. It shows where temperate forests and other biomes are located.

2. Look at the places where forest biomes are found. Compare them with the same places on a map of the world or on a world globe.

3. On which continents do temperate forests exist? Are there any continents that do not have a temperate forest biome?

4. Find where you live on a world map. Using Figure 1, find the biome where you live.

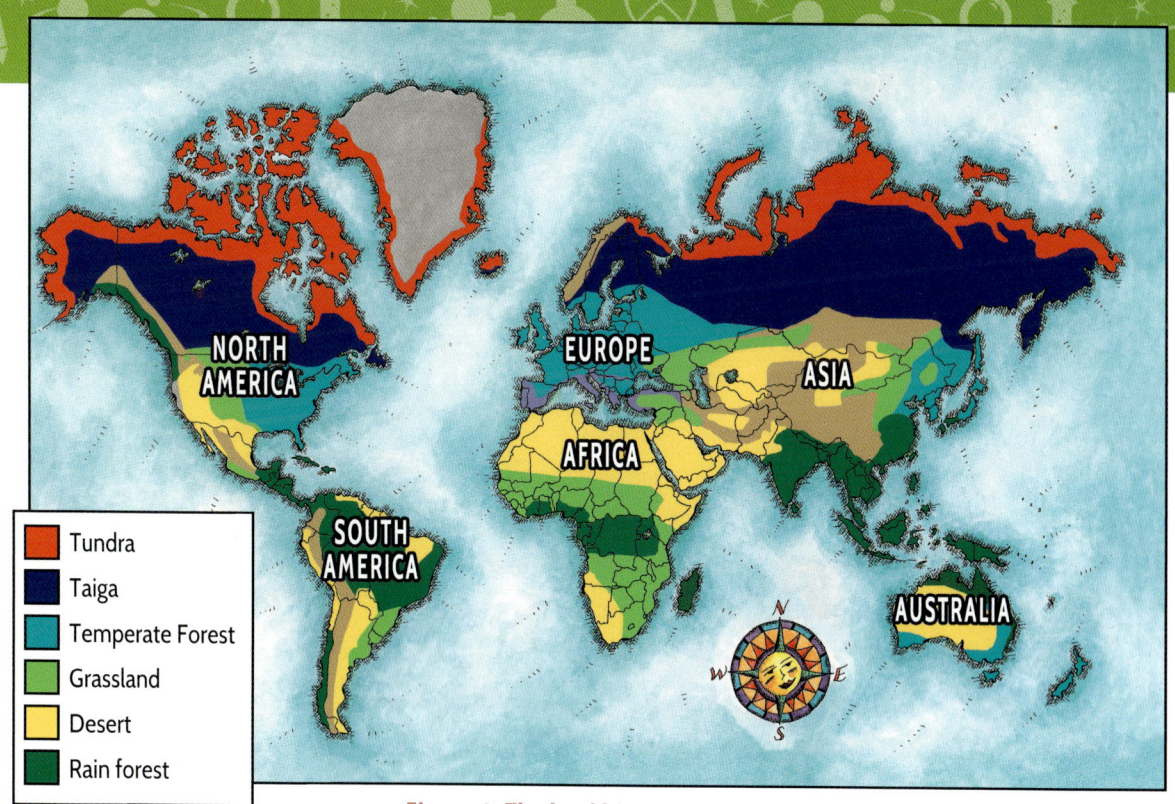

Figure 1. The land biomes of the world

What's Going On?

You compared the map of biomes in Figure 1 with a map of the world. You could see that temperate forests are found in North America, Europe, Asia, and Australia. There are no significant temperate forests in South America, Africa, or Antarctica.

By a similar comparison, you could see in which type of biome you live. You may think the map of biomes for your home is wrong. The map shows what is true for much of the region where you live, not every part of it. For example, the author lives on Cape Cod in Massachusetts. The biome map indicates that he lives in a temperate forest biome. However, the outer end of Cape Cod is like a desert. It is covered by sand dunes. Also, while forest covers much of Cape Cod, the trees are shorter than in a typical temperate forest. This is caused by the strong winds and salt air coming off the Atlantic Ocean.

2. A Climatogram of a City (20 minutes)

What's the Plan?
Let's make a climatogram for Nashville, Tennessee.

What You Do

WHAT YOU NEED:
- graph paper or computer
- pen or pencil
- Table 1

1. Use graph paper to make a climatogram for Nashville. The climatogram will show Nashville's average monthly temperature and rainfall. Figure 2 shows what a climatogram looks like. Months of the year are plotted along the horizontal axis. Rainfall is shown along the left vertical axis, temperature along the right vertical axis.

   Use the data in Table 1 to make the climatogram for Nashville.

Table 1. Monthly average temperatures and rainfall for Nashville, Tenn.

	Jan.	Feb.	Mar.	Apr.	May	Jun.	Jul.	Aug.	Sept.	Oct.	Nov.	Dec.
Temp. (°C)	4.2	5.7	10.3	15.4	20.5	24.8	26.6	25.9	22.6	16.4	9.9	5.3
Rainfall (in.)	4.6	4.1	5.1	4.2	4.1	3.9	3.9	3.4	3.3	2.5	3.6	4.1

2. What is the approximate average temperature for one year in Nashville?

3. What is the approximate total average rainfall for one year in Nashville?

4. Are Nashville's temperatures and rainfall normal for a temperate forest biome? Does Nashville have warm summers and cold winters? Does it have 30 to 80 inches of rain?

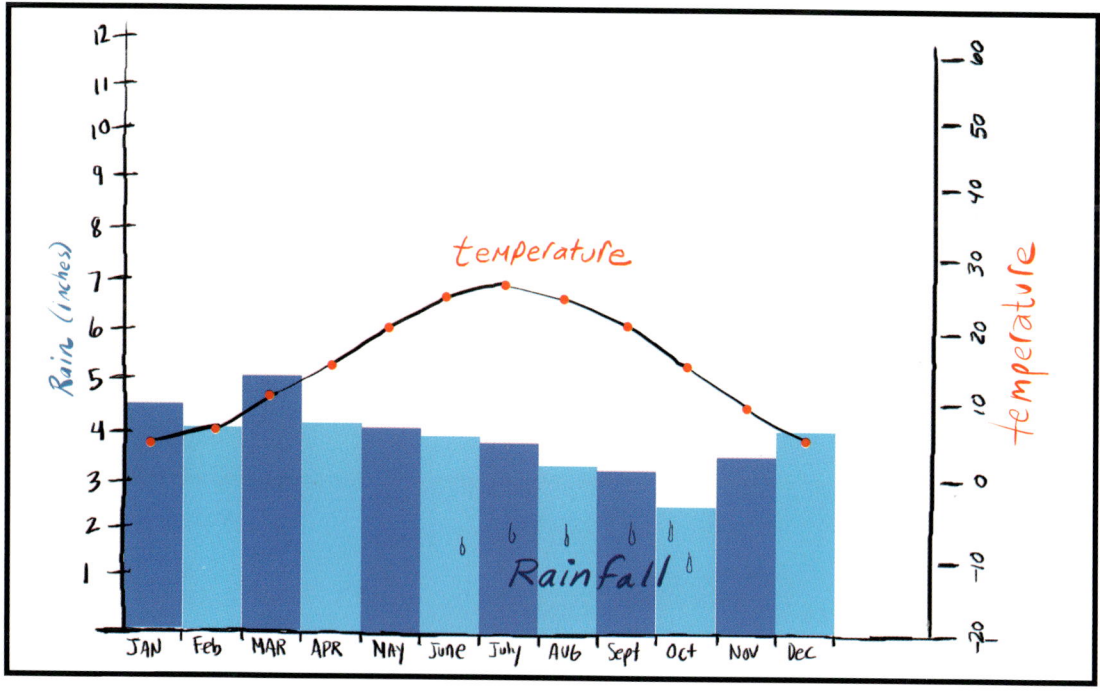

Figure 2. This is a sample climatogram. Now you can make your own for Nashville, Tenn.

What's Going On?

Your climatogram should show Nashville's average monthly temperature and rainfall in a graphical way. The approximate total rainfall in Nashville is 46.8 inches. The approximate average annual temperature is 15.6°C (60°F). These numbers are normal for a temperate forest biome.

Keep Exploring–If You Have More Time!

- Prepare a climatogram of your city or town. Is your total yearly rainfall between 30 and 80 inches? Do you have cold winters and warm summers? Is your climate normal for a temperate forest biome? Of some other biome?

3. Using a Tree's Shadow to Measure Its Height
(30 minutes)

WHAT YOU NEED:
- sunshine
- partner
- tree
- yardstick
- measuring tape

What's the Plan?
Let's find a tree's height by using its shadow (Figure 3a).

What You Do

1. On a sunny day, measure and record the length, l, of a tree's shadow (Figure 3a).

2. As soon as possible, have a partner hold a yardstick upright (in a vertical position). Measure and record the length of the yardstick's shadow (Figure 3b).

3. Calculate the ratio of the yardstick's height to the length of its shadow. For example, if the shadow is 18 inches long, the ratio is 2:

$$\frac{36 \text{ inches}}{18 \text{ inches}} = 2$$

4. Calculate and record the height of the tree. The ratio of the tree's height to the length of its shadow will be the same as it was for the yardstick. For example, assume you found that the ratio of the yardstick's height to the length of its shadow was 2. Similarly, if the tree's shadow is 15 feet long, its height is 30 feet.

Figure 3. a) Measure and record the length of a tree's shadow. b) Measure and record the length of a yardstick's shadow. c) The angle, a, that the sun's light rays make with the tree is the same as the angle the rays make with the yardstick.

What's Going On?

The sun's rays make the same angle (a) with the tree as they do with the yardstick (Figure 3c). Therefore, the tree, the yardstick, and their shadows form two similar triangles. The ratio of the yardstick's length (36 in) to its shadow will be the same as the ratio of the tree's height to its shadow. If you don't believe it, draw two right triangles like those in Figure 3c. Then measure the sides and find the ratios of their altitudes and bases.

Your measurements of the shadows must be made quickly. The shadows' lengths change as the sun moves across the sky.

Keep Exploring–If You Have More Time!

- Use shadows to measure the length of a flagpole.

- Use shadows to measure the height of a building.

- Measure the height of the same tree at different times of day. How well do the measurements agree?

4. Another Way to Measure a Tree's Height (30 minutes)

WHAT YOU NEED:
- a partner
- tall tree
- tape measure
- pencil

What's the Plan?

Let's measure a tree's height with a method used by artists.

What You Do

1. Ask a partner to stand next to the tree you plan to measure. You should stand about 20 meters (60 to 70 feet) from the tree.

2. Hold a pencil upright at arm's length as shown in Figure 4. Line up the top of the pencil with the top of your friend's head. Hold the pencil steady. Move your thumb down the pencil until it is in line with the bottom of your partner's feet. The distance between your thumb and the top of the pencil represents your partner's height. It is his or her height as seen from a distance of about 20 meters.

3. Next, decide how many of your partner's heights equal the tree's height. Do that by moving the pencil upward one partner height at a time (Figure 4). Count the number of partner heights that match the tree's height.

   How tall is your partner? Knowing your partner's height, you can make a good estimate of the tree's height. For example, suppose your partner is 1.5 meters (4 feet 11 inches) tall. Suppose, too, that the tree, according to your pencil measurement, is ten times taller than your partner. The height of the tree will be roughly 15 meters: 10 x 1.5 m = 15 m (49 feet).

Figure 4. The drawing shows the artist's method of estimating the height of a tree. In the drawing, the tree is seven times as tall as the person standing next to it.

What's Going On?

Artists use this method to ensure good perspective in their paintings or drawings. It is a good way to estimate the height of any tall object.

Keep Exploring–If You Have More Time!

- Measure the circumference of a tree's trunk. How can you use your measurement to find the tree's diameter?

- Measure the trunk diameter and height of a number of trees. Can you estimate the height of a tree by knowing the diameter of its trunk?

- Are some tree species consistently taller than other species?

5. Seasons in a Temperate Forest (30 minutes)

WHAT YOU NEED:
- flashlight
- globe

What's the Plan?
Let's see why temperate forests in the United States have seasons.

What You Do

1. In a dark room, shine a flashlight on a world globe. The light from the flashlight represents some of the sun's rays (not the entire sun). Shine the light perpendicular to a point on the Tropic of Capricorn (Figure 5a). Choose a point south of the temperate forest biome in the United States. (The Tropic of Capricorn is an imaginary line that goes around Earth 23.5° south of the equator.) On the first day of winter, the sun follows a path along and directly above the Tropic of Capricorn.

2. Move the flashlight slowly upward. Do not change the direction of its beam. Keep it parallel to its original direction. (Rays of sunlight reaching Earth are very nearly parallel.) Stop when its light falls on the U.S. forest biome. The light shining on the forest biome no longer makes a circular pattern of light. The beam is now spread out over a much wider area.

3. Continue to move the flashlight farther north along the globe. Do not change the direction of its beam. Notice that no light reaches the north pole region. It remains dark throughout the winter.

4. Move the flashlight so that it points directly at the Tropic of Cancer, an imaginary line that goes around Earth 23.5° north of the equator. On

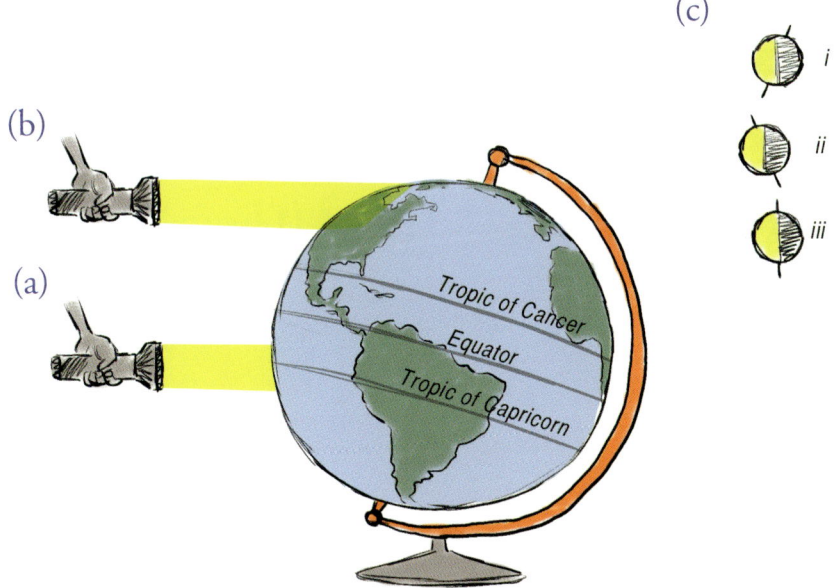

Figure 5. a) Shine a flashlight so its light strikes the Tropic of Capricorn at 90 degrees.
b) Without changing the light beam's direction, move it upward until the light falls on the U.S. temperate forest biome.
c) i) Winter sun ii) Summer sun iii) Spring and fall sun

the first day of summer, the sun follows a path along and directly above the Tropic of Cancer.

5. Move the flashlight slowly northward on the globe. Do not change the beam's direction. Stop when its light falls on the U.S. forest biome. As you can see, the beam shining on the forest biome makes a nearly circular pattern of light. The same light energy is spread over much less area than it was when the winter "sun" (flashlight) was over the Tropic of Capricorn.

What's Going On?

The more intense summer sunlight provides more warmth to the forest biome in the summer. In the winter, the less intense light allows the air temperature to fall.

One Hour or Less

These experiments take about an hour. You will find they are worth every minute.

6. How Old Was That Tree? (1 hour)

What's the Plan?
Let's see how we can find the age of a tree.

What You Do

WHAT YOU NEED:
- an adult
- tree stump, post, or fallen limb
- saw (optional)
- sandpaper (optional)

1. The photograph on page 23 shows the top of a tree stump. The stump is what's left of the tree's trunk after the tree is cut down. You can find the approximate age of a tree by counting the annual rings. How old was this tree?

2. Look for the stump of a tree. Count the rings. What was the approximate age of the tree before it was cut down? How can you tell in which years the tree grew a lot? How can you tell the years in which the tree grew very little?

   If you can't find a stump, look for a post. The rings across the top of the post may be visible. Approximately how old was the tree when it was cut down to make posts?

3. If you can't find a stump or a post, look for a large fallen limb. **Under adult supervision**, use a saw to cut across the limb. You should be able to see rings. If not, use sandpaper to smooth the wood. How old was the branch?

4. To find a tree's age by counting rings, the author used the words "approximate age." Why the approximate age?

The rings in stumps show the tree's approximate age.

What's Going On?

A tree adds a new ring every year. Each ring has two parts. The wider, lighter part is the spring-wood. It is made of cells that are added in the spring. A tree usually grows most rapidly in the spring when there's lots of water. The thinner, darker part of the ring, the summer-wood, is formed during the rest of the year. That's when the tree grows slowly because less water is available. Wide rings indicate a good year for growth.

The term "approximate" was used because sometimes a summer hurricane or tornado tears the leaves off trees. When the leaves grow back, a second ring appears as new growth takes place. The tree will show two rings for that year.

Keep Exploring–If You Have More Time!

- How do the ages of branches at the bottom and top of a tree compare?

7. Leaf Anatomy (1 hour)

> **WHAT YOU NEED:**
> - leaves from several different species of trees

What's the Plan?
Let's look at different leaves and see how they are the same or different.

What You Do

1. Collect several leaves from the same tree, such as a maple. Also, collect leaves from different species of trees. Can you find simple and compound leaves (Figure 6a)? Do all the leaves from a single tree have the same basic shape? How about leaves from trees of different species?

2. Notice the narrow rigid lines that give a leaf its shape and firmness. They are called veins. What function do you think they serve?

3. Veins are often either palmate, such as maple or sassafras leaves, or pinnate, such as oak or Japanese Cherry leaves (Figure 6b). Can you find other leaves with palmate veins? Can you find other leaves with pinnate veins?

Maple leaves

What's Going On?
Leaves from the same tree will all have the same basic shape and vein structure. Leaves from trees of different species probably will have a different shape and vein structure. However, the shapes

Oak leaves

and vein arrangement may be quite similar if the trees are closely related. You would surely recognize the similarity of leaves from sugar and Norway maples.

The veins in leaves connect to the tree's branches. They carry water and minerals to the leaf's cells. They also carry food manufactured in the leaf cells to other parts of the tree such as the trunk and roots. Your veins only carry blood to your heart. Arteries transport blood away from your heart. Leaf veins carry fluid both to and from the leaf's cells.

Figure 6. a) Leaves may be compound, having a number of leaflets, or they may be simple, consisting of a single blade. b) The veins in leaves may be pinnate or palmate.

Keep Exploring–If You Have More Time!

- Find a way to estimate the total number of leaves on a tree.

- Find a way to preserve and display colorful autumn leaves.

8. Testing Wood for Hardness (1 hour)

What's the Plan?

Let's test different kinds of wood for hardness. One way to do this is to drive identical nails into different woods. As you might expect, it is easier to drive a nail into softwood than into hardwood.

What You Do

1. Obtain a hammer and a few long, identical nails.

2. To avoid hitting your fingers, hold the nail you are going to hammer with pliers. Remove a small bit of bark from a pine or fir tree's trunk. Then drive one of the nails into the tree.

3. Drive the other nails into different trees. You might try oak, maple, hickory, beech, birch, fir, or whatever tree species are available. Ask an adult to help you, or use a guide-to-trees book to identify the trees. Which woods seem to be hard woods? Which are soft woods? How can you tell?

4. Another method would be to obtain pieces of oak, pine, and other types of wood boards. Use boards of the same thickness. Place one of the boards on a work bench or on a concrete block. Hold the nail with pliers. Use a hammer to drive an identical nail into each kind of wood. Which seem to be hard woods? Which are soft woods?

WHAT YOU NEED:
- an adult
- hammer
- a few long, identical nails
- pliers
- a variety of trees: oak, maple, ash, hickory, beech, birch, pine, cedar, fir or whatever species are available
- a guide to trees
- oak, pine, and other types of wood boards of the same thickness
- work bench or concrete block
- safety glasses

What's Going On?

You probably found it more difficult to drive a nail into a hardwood tree, such as an oak, than into softer wood, such as pine. Hardwoods include beech, cherry, hickory, maple, oak, and others. Softwoods include cedar, fir, pine, spruce, and others.

Keep Exploring–If You Have More Time!

- Wooden baseball bats used in the major leagues are made of ash. Do you think ash is a hardwood or a softwood? Do an experiment to find out.

- Are hardwoods more dense (heavier for the same volume) than softwoods? Do or design experiments to find out.

Two Hours or More

Are you a budding scientist with some more time on your hands? The next experiments take from two hours to two months. It will be time well spent!

9. The Density of Hardwood and Softwood (1 to 2 hours)

What's the Plan?

Let's compare the densities of hardwood and softwood. Density is the mass of an object divided by its volume. Often, the mass is measured in grams (g) and the volume is measured in cubic centimeters (cm^3). Then the density would be measured in grams per cubic centimeter (g/cm^3). It might also be measured in g/mL. A milliliter (mL) and a cubic centimeter (cm^3) have the same volume. Usually, milliliters are used with liquids.

What You Do

1. Cut a cylindrical piece of wood from the branch of a conifer (softwood), such as a pine tree. Do the same for a broad-leaf hardwood tree, such as a maple, birch, or oak.

2. Weigh and record the mass of the softwood and the mass of the hardwood.

WHAT YOU NEED:
- an adult
- branches of softwood and hardwood trees
- saw or knife
- scale
- pencil and notebook
- measuring tape
- water
- graduated cylinder or measuring cup
- long pin
- hardwood and softwood boards

28

3. If the samples are nearly uniform cylinders, you can find their volumes using math. Measure and record the length (L) and diameter (D) of each sample. Calculate their volumes (V) using the following formula: $V = \pi \times R^2 \times L$. Let $\pi = 3.14$. R is the radius (half the diameter).

4. If the samples are not uniform cylinders, find their volumes by displacement of water. Add some water to a graduated cylinder or metric measuring cup. Add enough water so that the wood can be completely submerged in water. Record the volume of water.

Pine trees

5. Place one of the wood samples in the graduated cylinder or measuring cup. Use a long pin to submerge the wood. The wood will displace a volume of water equal to its volume. Record the new volume of water plus wood.

6. Subtract the original volume of water to find the volume of the wood. For example, if the water is now 90 cm^3 (or mL) and it was 40 cm^3 before, the volume of the wood is 50 cm^3.

7. Repeat your measurements for the other sample.

8. Calculate the density of each wood. Which wood is more dense?

    If time permits, compare the densities of living wood with seasoned wood. Wood found in lumber used for building or making furniture is seasoned wood.

9. Obtain a sample of a hardwood board, such as oak or maple and a softwood board, such as pine or fir. **Ask an adult** to cut some samples for you. A good size for a sample would be about 10 cm x 10 cm x 5 cm (4 in x 4 in x 2 in).

10. Weigh the samples and record their masses.

11. Measure the length, width, and height of each sample. Record those dimensions.

12. Calculate the volumes of the two samples. Remember, volume equals length x width x thickness.

13. Use the mass and volume of each sample to calculate their densities. Is seasoned hardwood or softwood more dense? How do the densities compare with the densities of the living hardwood and softwood that you measured earlier?

What's Going On?

You probably found that living hardwood is more dense than living softwood. The same was probably true of the seasoned wood. Seasoned hardwood lumber is more dense than seasoned softwood lumber.

Living wood contains water. Seasoning consists of drying the wood—letting the water in the wood evaporate. Once the fraction of water in the wood is reduced to 10 percent or less, the wood is less likely to warp (bend upon further drying). The loss of water makes the wood less dense. Therefore, you probably found the seasoned wood was less dense than the living wood.

Maple tree

Keep Exploring–If You Have More Time!

- Find an oddly shaped object that is made of wood. Design and do an experiment to find the density of the wooden object. Use that information to identify the wood from which the object was made or decide if it is made of hardwood or softwood.

10. Chromatography and Leaf Pigments (2 hours)

What's the Plan?

Although most leaves appear to be green, they often contain other pigments. Let's see if we can separate the colored pigments in leaves. But first, let's investigate chromatography. Then we'll use chromatography to try to separate leaf pigments.

To see how chromatography works, let's separate the pigments found in inks.

What You Do

1. Collect several different varieties of black, felt-tip pens.

2. Add about 2 cm (1 in) of water to a long, narrow tray or plastic dish. Arrange a long stick or ruler so that it is about 15 cm (6 in) above the water. Use books to support the ends of the stick.

3. Cut strips from white coffee filters or blotting paper. Make the strips about 15 cm (6 in) long and 2 cm (1 in) wide. You'll need one strip for each pen.

4. Using scissors, cut one end of each strip into an arrow shape.

WHAT YOU NEED:
- several different black felt-tip pens
- water
- long, narrow tray or plastic dish
- long stick or ruler
- books or other heavy objects
- white coffee filters or blotting paper
- scissors
- ruler
- tape
- tall jars with covers
- paper
- leaf
- dull pencil
- rubbing alcohol
- tall glass
- chair or cabinet

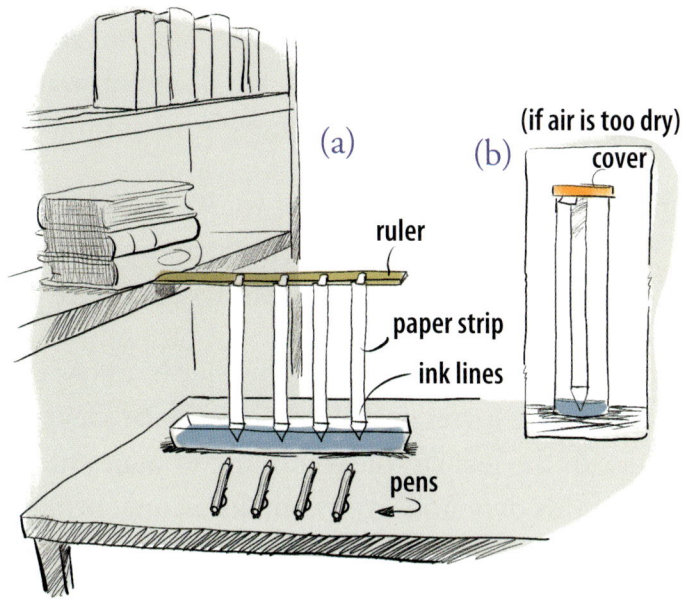

Figure 7. a) Paper strips marked with ink from different felt-tipped pens are ready for paper chromatography.
b) In dry air, strips may need to be enclosed.

5. Just above the arrow head on one strip, draw a black line with one of the pens.

6. Use tape to hang the strip from the long stick. Only the tip of the arrow should touch the water. Place the pen used to mark the strip next to the strip.

7. Mark each remaining strip with a different pen. Hang each strip from the long stick. Be sure that only the tip of the arrow touches the water. Place the pen used to mark each strip next to the strip as shown (Figure 7a).

8. Water will move up the strips. It will carry the ink pigments upward. Some pigments will move farther than others. This will cause colors to separate. Which colors were the pigments in the various inks?

9. If the air is very dry, hang the strips from covers resting on tall jars. (See Figure 7b.) The cover will prevent water from evaporating.

10. Some inks do not dissolve in water. Colors in these inks will not move up the strip. For such inks, use rubbing alcohol in place of water. Now let's try to separate the pigments in leaves using chromatography.

1. Cut a strip of filter paper or blotter paper about 20 to 30 cm (8 to 12 inches) long and 2 cm (1 in) wide. You can make such a strip by opening a white coffee filter and cutting along the dotted lines shown in Figure 8a.

2. Place the strip on a sheet of paper. Make a line of leaf pigments across the strip about 2 cm from what will be its lower end. To do this, place a leaf on the strip. Using a dull pencil, rub the leaf so it leaves a line of pigment on the paper strip (Figure 8b). Do this over and over to make a concentrated line of pigment on the paper. The pencil will break through the leaf, so you will have to move the leaf after each rubbing.

3. Add rubbing alcohol to a tall glass. The liquid should be about 2 cm deep.

4. Carefully hang the paper strip. Use tape to hang the strip from a chair, cabinet, or other suitable structure. The lower tip of the strip below the line of pigment should dip a very short distance into the alcohol (Figure 8c). Use paper to cover as much of the open top of the glass as possible.

5. Allow 30 to 50 minutes for the alcohol to carry the pigments up the paper strip. When the alcohol stops rising farther up the strip, remove the strip. Hang it up to dry.

What's Going On?

The pigments move up the paper at different rates and become separated. Leaves contain chlorophyll, a green pigment vital to the process of photosynthesis. Many leaves also contain yellow and orange pigments. You may have seen these pigments as well.

If you do this experiment in the fall, the leaves may be turning color. You may not find any chlorophyll. Less light and cooler temperatures reduce the production of chlorophyll. Instead of a green pigment, you may see yellow, orange, and red pigments. Those other pigments are also there in the summer but are masked by the more abundant green chlorophyll. Chromatography can separate the pigments and make them all visible. The pigments you see will depend on the kind of tree from which the leaf came.

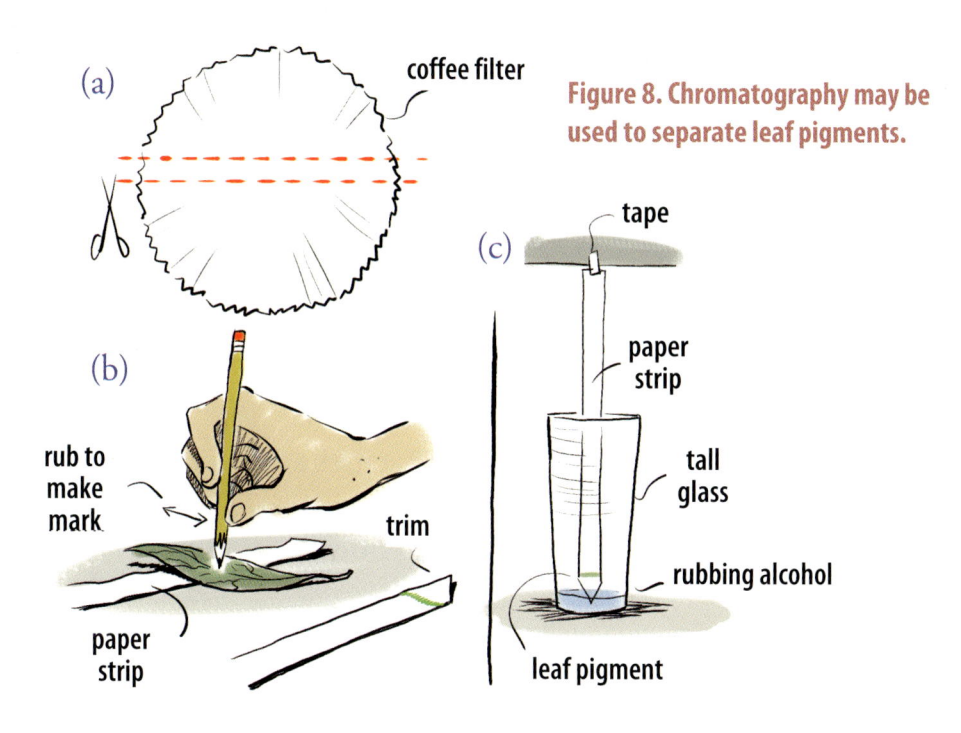

Figure 8. Chromatography may be used to separate leaf pigments.

Keep Exploring–If You Have More Time!

- Do food colorings contain more than one colored chemical? Do experiments to find out.

- Do other colored inks (blue, green, red, etc.) contain more than one pigment? How about India ink?

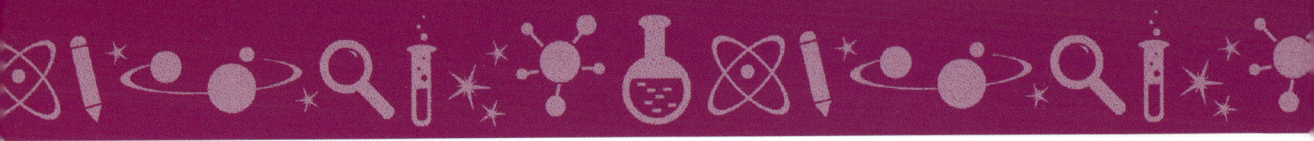

11. Leaves: A Tree's Food Factory (2 days)

> **WHAT YOU NEED:**
> - an adult
> - paper clip
> - black construction paper
> - geranium plant
> - sunny day
> - gloves
> - safety glasses
> - tongs
> - pan
> - stove
> - water
> - alcohol
> - small jar
> - saucer
> - tincture of iodine

What's the Plan?

Let's do an experiment to see if food is produced in a leaf. Starch, a food, turns dark blue when iodine is added to it.

What You Do

1. Use a paper clip to fix a folded piece of black construction paper over both sides of a geranium leaf as shown in Figure 9. Be careful! Don't damage the leaf when you attach the paper. Do this in the morning on a bright sunny day. Then lots of light will fall on the leaf during most of the day.

2. In the late afternoon, pick the leaf from the plant. Bring it indoors and remove the cover.

3. Put on gloves and safety glasses. Hold the leaf's stem with tongs. **Under adult supervision**, immerse the rest of the leaf into a pan of boiling water on a stove. Hold the leaf under the boiling water for about one minute. The heat will break open cell walls within the leaf.

4. Turn off the stove because you are going to use alcohol. Alcohol is flammable!

To remove the green pigment (chlorophyll) from the leaf, put the limp leaf in a small jar of alcohol. Leave it overnight.

5. The next morning, you will see the alcohol has turned green. Much of the chlorophyll has been removed from the leaf. In a saucer, mix approximately equal amounts of tincture of iodine and water (about 5 mL of each will do). REMEMBER: IODINE IS POISONOUS. HANDLE IT CAREFULLY!

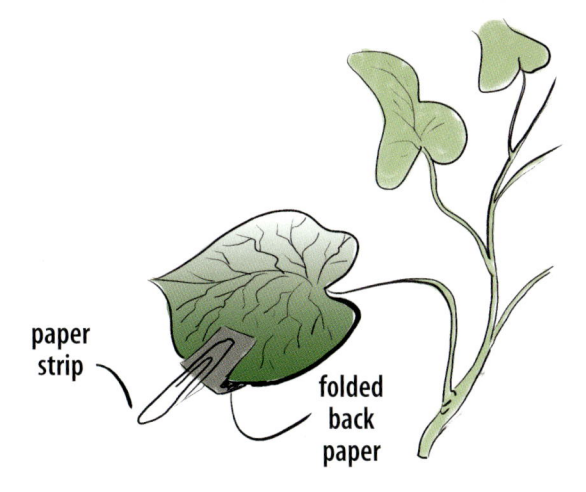

Figure 9. Use a paper clip to fasten a folded piece of black construction paper to a geranium leaf. Light will not be able to reach the leaf cells covered by the paper. It will reach other cells in the leaf.

6. Rinse the leaf in warm water. Then spread it out and place it in the iodine-water mixture. The leaf will turn a dark blue-black color. Notice that one area of the leaf is much lighter than the rest. Can you identify that region? In which area of the leaf did photosynthesis not take place? How can you tell?

What's Going On?

Chlorophyll enables plants to use light energy to carry on photosynthesis. Photosynthesis is a process by which plants change carbon dioxide and water to oxygen and sugar. The sugar produced in a leaf is changed to starch and stored. You used the common test for starch (iodine) to show that food is produced in leaves when light is present. Starch turns a blue-black color in iodine. The covered part of the leaf was not blue-black. Those cells produced no starch because light is needed for photosynthesis to occur.

12. Transpiration: How Trees Lose Water in Warm Weather (2 days)

WHAT YOU NEED:
- sunny day
- 2 clear, 30-gallon plastic bags
- broad-leaf tree
- stone
- twisties
- tree with needlelike leaves

What's the Plan?

We know trees need water to live. Let's do an experiment to see if trees lose water.

What You Do

1. Begin this experiment early on a clear, warm, sunny day in the spring or summer.

2. Place a clear, 30-gallon plastic bag over a small, sunlit branch of a broad-leaf tree, such as a maple. Put a stone in the bag to make it sag from the branch (Figure 10). Use one or more twisties to seal the open end of the bag around the branch.

3. Carry out the same experiment on a tree with needlelike leaves, such as a pine tree.

4. Leave the bags attached to the branches until the next day. Then examine the contents of the bags. Has water collected in either or both bags? If so, does one bag have more water than the other?

What's Going On?

Trees lose water through openings (stomata) in their leaves. The process is called transpiration. As you probably found, the broad-leaf (hardwood) tree lost more water than the softwood tree (pine). This is not surprising. The broad leaves have a much larger surface area than the needle-like leaves of a conifer. The large surface provides water molecules with more opportunities to escape into the air. An apple tree, for example, may lose 1,800 gallons of water during one growing season. Transpiration is one of the main reasons soils become dry. Soil water absorbed by tree roots moves up the tree and escapes through the leaves.

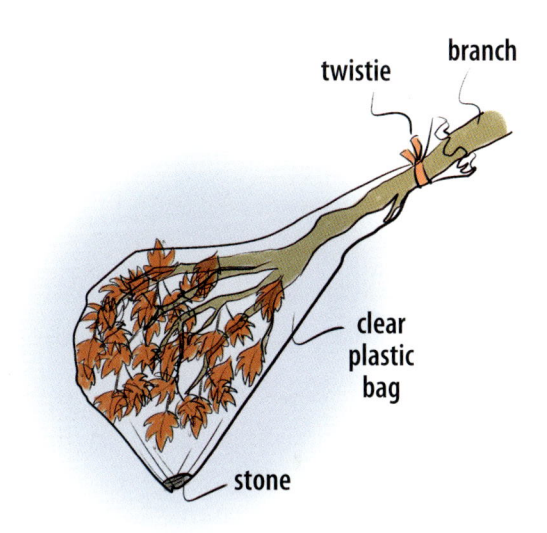

Figure 10. Will water collect in the sealed bag that surrounds the leaves?

Keep Exploring–If You Have More Time!

- Do experiments to see how transpiration is affected by one or more of the following: (a) wind; (b) humidity; (c) temperature; (d) sunlight; (e) shade; (f) darkness.

13. Transpiration: Do Trees Lose Water in Cold Weather? (2 days)

What's the Plan?
Trees need water to live. Let's do an experiment to see if trees lose water in cold weather.

WHAT YOU NEED:
- clear, cold, sunny day
- clear, 30-gallon plastic bag
- broad-leaf tree
- stone
- twisties
- tree with needlelike leaves

What You Do

1. Begin this experiment early on a clear, cold, sunny day in the late fall or winter.

2. Put a clear, 30-gallon plastic bag over a small branch of a broad-leaf tree, such as a maple. Put a stone in the bag to make it sag from the branch (Figure 11a). Use one or more twisties to seal the bag to the branch.

3. Carry out the same experiment on a tree with needle-like leaves, such as a pine tree (Figure 11b).

4. Leave the bags attached to the branches until the next day. Then examine the contents of the bags. Has water collected in either or both bags? If so, does one bag have more water than the other?

What's Going On?
Trees lose water through openings (stomata) in their leaves. The process is called transpiration. But in winter, deciduous trees, such as maples and birches, have no leaves.

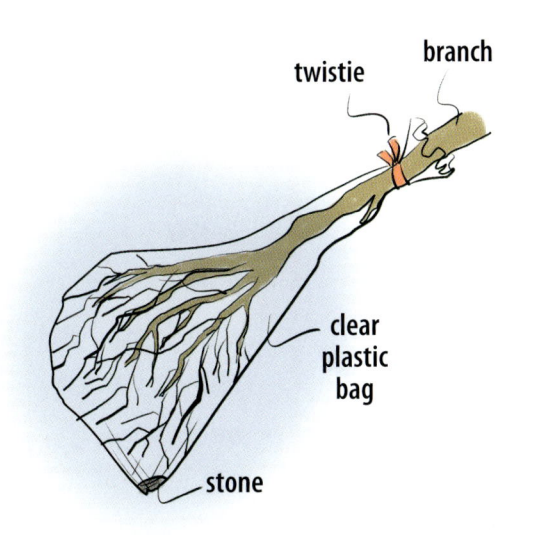

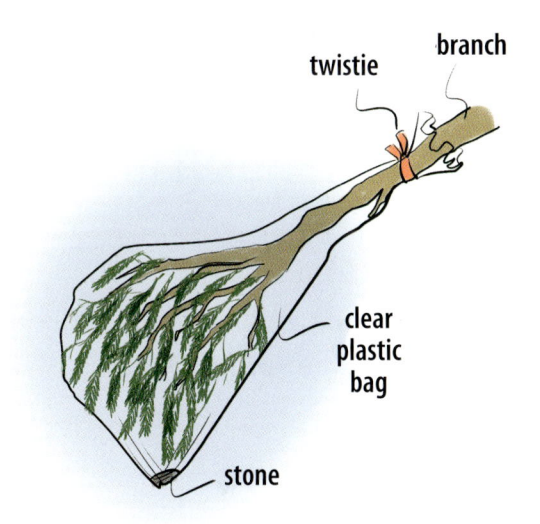

Figure 11. a) Seal a bag over a bare branch of a deciduous, hardwood tree. Will water collect in the bag?

b) Seal a bag over a branch of a conifer. Will there be water in the bag after 24 hours?

As you probably found, the leafless deciduous tree lost very little, if any, water. It had no leaves. There were no leaf openings through which water vapor could escape. Conifers, however, keep their needlelike leaves in winter. You probably found that some water droplets could be seen on the plastic bag. Transpiration does take place in conifers during cold months.

Ground water is usually plentiful in the spring. Transpiration is very limited in hardwood trees during the winter. As a result, water has had time to be restored to the soil.

Keep Exploring—If You Have More Time!

- Do an experiment to compare the percentage of water in soil in winter and in summer.

14. Trees, Flowers, and Cones (1 to 2 months)

WHAT YOU NEED:
- **flowering trees and conifers**
- **water**
- **pine pollen**
- **microscope slide with cover slip**
- **microscope**

What's the Plan?
Let's look for flowers and cones that appear on trees in the spring.

What You Do
During the spring, leaves form from buds on broad-leaf trees such as maples and oaks. It is also when you will see flowers on the trees.

1. Look for flowers on trees. Many tree flowers are not bright and colorful, such as tulips, but they are flowers nevertheless. The photographs show flowers on maple and oak trees. Can you find flowers on these trees and others near your home?
   Spring is also the time when cones appear on conifers such as pine trees. There are two types of cones—male and female. Both types may be found on the same tree. There are smaller male cones and larger female cones.

2. Look for male cones and female cones on pine trees. Can you find them?

3. Also look for pine pollen later in the spring. Where pines are abundant, the yellow pollen may coat the ground. Pollen will be apparent around puddles as they dry.

Maple tree flowers

4. Add some pine pollen to a drop of water on a microscope slide. Add a cover slip.

5. Examine the pollen under a microscope. Does it look like the magnified pollen grains seen in the photograph?

Oak tree flowers

What's Going On?
The flowers of broad-leaf trees contain stamens tipped by anthers that produce pollen. The pollen falls on, or is carried by birds or insects to, a pistil. A pistil is part of a flower that contains an egg cell. The egg and sperm from the pollen unite to form a zygote (a tree embryo). The zygote becomes part of a seed that contains food for the embryo. The pistil surrounding the seed becomes the fruit that encloses the seed.

Pollen from the male conifer cones is carried by wind or gravity to the female cones. Later sperm cells produced in the pollen fertilize an egg in the female cone, giving rise to a seed. Conifers do not have flowers. Therefore, the seeds are not enclosed in a fruit.

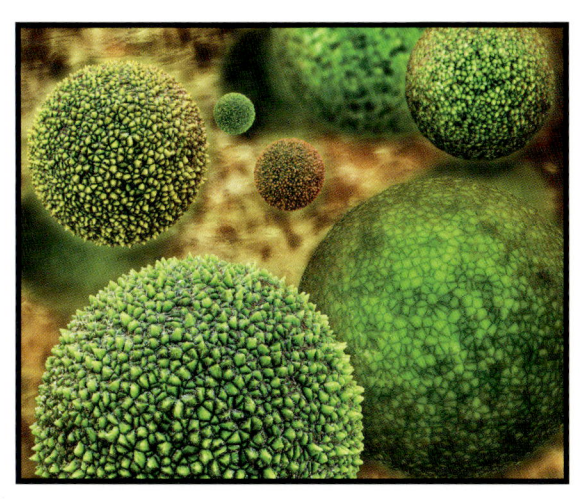

Birch pollen grains are shown in a 3-D rendering.

15. Trees, Flowers, Fruits, and Seeds
(1 to 2 months)

What's the Plan?

Let's look for the fruit of a maple, apple, or oak tree. Let's also search for the seeds in a female pine cone.

WHAT YOU NEED:
- **maple, apple, or oak tree**
- **pine tree**

What You Do

1. Once the flowers on a maple, apple, or oak tree appear, try to look at them each day. The base of a flower's pistil will become its fruit if the egg within the pistil is fertilized. The fruit of a maple tree is shown in the photograph below. Its propeller-like "wings" allow it to be carried by wind to soil where it may germinate.

2. Look for apple blossoms. Identify the pistils within the flowers. Continue to watch them. Tiny apples will appear at the base of the pistils soon after the trees blossom. When will apples be ready for you to eat?

3. Oak flowers take much longer to form their fruit, which is the familiar acorn. In late summer or early autumn acorns will fall from oak trees. Within the acorn is the seed. Break open an acorn and you'll see the seed.

Maple tree fruits

4. Watch the female cones on pine trees. In late summer, the cones open. You can see winged seeds on the cones' scales. If they fall and are carried by wind to suitable soil, they may germinate.

Oak tree fruit are called acorns.

What's Going On?

Should a maple seed land in suitable soil, it may germinate and grow.

Often a squirrel will bury an acorn and forget its location. Given the right soil and moisture, the seed may give rise to a baby oak tree.

It takes several months for an apple to mature. By late summer or early fall, apples are ready to be eaten.

Apple tree flowers

Keep Exploring–If You Have More Time!

- In a garden, watch the flowers of tomatoes and squash turn into fruit. Squash plants bear either staminate (male) or pistillate (female) flowers. Try to identify each kind.

Apple tree fruit

45

Words to Know

biome—A region of Earth with a characteristic climate and species of plants and animals.

chlorophyll—A green pigment found in green plants. It serves as a catalyst in the conversion of light energy to chemical energy during photosynthesis.

climatogram—A graph that shows annual monthly rainfall and temperature for a particular place on Earth, such as a city or town.

chromatography—A method of separating substances, such as pigments, by means of the rate at which they move though a medium.

deciduous trees—Trees that lose their leaves during cold weather or during a dry season.

density—The mass of something divided by its volume. For example, the density of water is 1.0 gram/milliliter (g/mL).

flower—The reproductive part of many plants.

fruit—The ripened ovary of a flower. It contains the plant's seeds.

photosynthesis—A process by which green plants manufacture food. Leaf cells, using chlorophyll as a catalyst, combine carbon dioxide, water, and the energy from sunlight to make food for the plant. During the process, oxygen is also formed.

stomata—The openings in plant leaves that allow water to escape into the air.

transpiration—The loss of water by evaporation from a plant.

Tropic of Cancer—An imaginary line that goes around Earth 23.5° north of the equator. The sun is directly above this latitude on the first day of summer in the Northern Hemisphere.

Tropic of Capricorn— An imaginary line that goes around Earth 23.5° south of the equator. The sun is directly above this latitude on the first day of winter in the Northern Hemisphere.

veins—The support tissue in leaves that carries water and nutrients to the cells of a leaf.

Further Reading

Books

Allaby, Michael. *Temperate Forests*. New York: Chelsea House, 2006.

Bardhan-Quallen, Sudipta. *Championship Science Fair Projects: 100 Sure-to-Win Experiments*. New York: Sterling, 2005.

Callery, Sean. *Forest*. New York: Kingfisher, 2012.

Davis, Barbara. *Biomes and Ecosystems*. Milwaukee: Gareth Stevens Publishers, 2007.

Hurtig, Jennifer. *Deciduous Forests*. New York: Weigl Publishers, 2011.

Pyers, Greg. *Biodiversity of Woodlands*. New York: Marshall Cavendish Benchmark, 2011.

Wojahn, Rebecca Hogue, and Donald Wojahn. *A Temperate Forest Food Chain: A Who-Eats-What Adventure in North America*. Minneapolis: Lerner, 2009.

Web Sites

Temperate Forest—Kids Do Ecology
<kids.nceas.ucsb.edu/biomes/temperateforest.html>

Temperate Forest
<www.globio.org/glossopedia/article.aspx?art_id=3>

Index

A
acorns, 44–45
animals, 6
annual rings in trees, 22–23
apples, 44–45

C
chlorophyll, 5, 34–35, 37
chromatography, 32–35
climatograms, 14–15
cones, 42–45
conifers, 5, 38–43
conservation, 7

D
deciduous trees, 5–6
density measurement, 28–31

E
experiments, designing, 8–9

F
fall colors, 5–6
flowers, 42–45

H
hardwoods, 26–31
height measurement
    artist method, 18–19
    tree's shadow, 16–17
    height to length ratio formula, 16
hibernation, 6

L
leaves
    anatomy, 24–25
    food production, 36–37
    pigments, 32–35
    transpiration, 38–41

M
maps, using, 12–13
mass measurement, 28–31
mercury, 11

N
northern temperate zone, 6–7
notebooks, 11
nutrient cycle, 6

P
photosynthesis, 5, 34, 37
pollen, 42–43
precipitation, 6, 14–15

S
safety, 10–11
science fairs, 9–10
scientific method, 8–9
seasoning wood, 31
seasons, 20–21
softwoods, 26–31
starch production, 36–37

T
temperate forest, United States, 7
temperate forest biomes, 4–7
thermometers, 11
trees
    age measurement, 22–23
    density measurement, 28–31
    flowers, fruits, and seeds, 44–45
    flowers and cones, 42–45
    height measurement, 16–17
    transpiration, 38–41
    wood hardness testing, 26–27

V
veins in leaves, 24–25
volume measurement, 28–31

W
water displacement measurement, 29–30
wood hardness testing, 26–27

577.307 G RIN
Gardner, Robert,
Temperate forest experiments :8
 science experiments in one hour or les
RING
11/14